# STRAY TO STAR!

## A Shelter Dog Story

by Meish Goldish

illustrated by Frank Scherbarth

BEARPORT
PUBLISHING

New York, New York

**Credits**
Cover photo, © Eric Isselée/Shutterstock.

Publisher: Kenn Goin
Senior Editor: Joyce Tavolacci
Creative Director: Spencer Brinker

*Library of Congress Cataloging-in-Publication Data*

Names: Goldish, Meish, author.
Title: Stray to Star! A Shelter Dog Story / by Meish Goldish.
Description: New York, New York : Bearport Publishing, [2017] I Series: Hound
    Town Chronicles I Summary: Moving to Hound Town, a lonely boy's first
    friend is a brave dog.
Identifiers: LCCN 2016042371 (print) I LCCN 2016053146 (ebook) I ISBN
    9781684020164 (library) I ISBN 9781684020676 (ebook)
Subjects: I CYAC: Dogs—Fiction. I Friendship—Fiction. I Moving,
    Household—Fiction.
Classification: LCC PZ7.G56777 Lu 2017 (print) I LCC PZ7.G56777 (ebook) I DDC
    [Fic]—dc23
LC record available at https://lccn.loc.gov/2016042371

For more information, write to Bearport Publishing Company, Inc., 45 West 21st
Street, Suite 3B, New York, New York 10010. Printed in the United States of
America.

10 9 8 7 6 5 4 3 2 1

# CONTENTS

CHAPTER 1: **Rustling in the Bushes** . . . . . . . 4

CHAPTER 2: **At the Shelter** . . . . . . . . . . . . 10

CHAPTER 3: **A Friend's Help** . . . . . . . . . . . 16

CHAPTER 4: **Into the Woods** . . . . . . . . . . . 20

CHAPTER 5: **Stray to Star!** . . . . . . . . . . . . 26

What Do You Think?. . . . . . . . . . . . . . . . . . 30

Glossary. . . . . . . . . . . . . . . . . . . . . . . . . 31

About the Author. . . . . . . . . . . . . . . . . . . 32

About the Illustrator. . . . . . . . . . . . . . . . . 32

WELCOME TO **HOUND TOWN**

*A Doggone Nice Place to Live!*

Population:
25,000 people
20,000 dogs

# CHAPTER 1

# Rustling in the Bushes

It was a bright summer day. Cory Davis walked down the sidewalk in his new neighborhood, kicking a tiny pebble. The ten-year-old looked at a row of tidy houses. Each one had a square green lawn. He was hoping to spot a kid his age playing outside, but so far, no such luck.

Cory's family had just moved to Hound Town. But he already missed his old neighborhood and friends. If only Cory could make a new friend in town. Being quiet and shy didn't help. As Cory walked, he heard his mom's voice in his head: *Cory, you'll make new friends once school starts in September.* Sure, Cory thought. It's only July now. September seemed a lifetime away.

Cory walked a few more blocks. As he turned onto Howling Lane, he heard a rustling sound in some nearby bushes. Cory noticed a furry tail jutting out of the greenery. Then, suddenly, a scruffy brown animal popped out of the bushes. It was a smallish dog with messy brown and black fur.

Cory and the dog's eyes met. They both froze. The mutt had a small black nose, friendly eyes, and looked as if she had a slight smile

on her face. Not sure what to do, Cory stood perfectly still. Then with a soft voice he said, "Hey, there. What's your name? Are you lost?"

The dog tilted her head to the side as if she was listening.

Cory took a step forward. The dog backed up. "It's okay. Don't be afraid. I'm not going to hurt you," Cory said gently. The dog stopped. "Where's your owner?" Cory continued.

Slowly, he moved toward the scruffy dog, knelt down, and held out his hand so she could sniff it. After a few seconds, the pooch stepped forward and raised her wet black nose to Cory's fingers. Then Cory was able to stroke her head.

"You must belong to someone in the neighborhood," Cory said to the animal. "Your owner is going to miss you if you don't go home soon." The dog wasn't wearing a collar. And judging from her **matted** fur, it looked as if she hadn't been **groomed** in a while.

Cory petted the dog again. "So where did you come from, huh?" he asked. The dog simply stared at him and slowly wagged her shaggy tail.

Cory decided to go back to his house. He was sure the dog would disappear into the bushes when he walked away. Instead, the pup began to follow him. "Go back to your owner," Cory **commanded** as he shooed the dog away.

The shaggy dog slowed her **pace** but continued to trail the boy. Cory was a little nervous that she was following him. But he was also excited. Maybe this dog would be the friend he was searching for.

Cory arrived home and climbed onto the wide front porch of his family's gray two-story house. The dog was still behind him. "Mom! Dad! Look who followed me home," Cory called to his parents.

Cory's mom and dad appeared at the front door. "Who is *this*?" Mom asked with a smile.

"It's a dog I found," Cory said. "She's very friendly. She sniffed my hand and let me pet her." Then he paused and said, "I don't think she has a home."

Mom and Dad looked at each other. Dad had a serious look on his face. "How do you know this dog doesn't have an owner, Cory?"

"She isn't wearing a collar," Cory said. And her fur is all tangled. Then, he said **meekly**, "I was hoping maybe we could give her a home."

Mom said, "I don't know, Cory. We just moved here. And we never discussed getting a pet. It's a lot of responsibility. . . ."

"First things first," Dad interrupted. "Let's make sure she doesn't already have an owner. We can take her to the local **animal shelter** and try to find out more about her. Then we can discuss whether or not to keep her."

Cory could hardly wait to get into the car with the dog. "Come on, girl," he cried, carefully lifting the small animal in his arms. "We're going for a ride!"

# CHAPTER 2

# At the Shelter

During the car ride, Cory held the pup on his lap and petted her lovingly. The dog stuck her nose out the window and sniffed the warm air. As a gentle breeze blew across Cory's face, he dreamed about keeping his new friend.

On the way to the shelter, Mom and Dad checked telephone poles in the neighborhood for "Missing Dog" posters. They found only one, and it had a picture of a white poodle on it.

"Here we are," Dad announced as they arrived at a square brick building. "This is the Hound Town Animal Shelter."

As the Davis family walked inside, they immediately heard a **chorus** of dogs loudly barking. Cory couldn't believe how many dogs were at the shelter.

At the front desk, a shelter worker named Tara said, "Hi there. How can I help you?"

Cory could think only about all the dogs he was seeing and hearing. He suddenly said, "How many dogs are here? And where did they come from?"

"We care for about sixty dogs at the shelter," Tara said. The loud barking continued.

"We get them from lots of different places," Tara explained. "Sometimes pet owners become sick or too busy to care for their animals. Then they bring them here, and we feed and house them until someone **adopts** them."

Tara looked at the shaggy dog in Cory's arms. "Who's this little guy?"

Cory pulled the pup close to him. "I found her today near my house. I really want to keep her, but we don't know if she already has an owner."

"Okay," Tara said. She looked the animal over. "This dog is probably a **stray**. Unfortunately, people sometimes let their unwanted pets loose on the street."

Tara studied a sheet of paper on her desk. "Nobody has reported a missing dog fitting your dog's description," she said. "Let's check to see if she has a **microchip**. That can help us find out if she has an owner."

Tara reached for a special scanner and placed it just behind the dog's shoulder. "Nope, this dog doesn't have a chip," said Tara.

Turning to the family, Tara said, "Unless someone comes looking for her, you're free to keep her. But, first, we'd like to check to make sure she's healthy and that she's been **spayed**."

"Mom, Dad, can we keep her? Pretty *pleaassse*? I'll feed her and clean up after her every day, I promise," Cory begged.

Cory's parents looked at each other. "She does have a sweet **temperament**," Dad said. Mom nodded. Then Mom turned to Cory. "Caring for her will be a lot of work, Cory. It's a big **commitment**. . . . But we can see how much you love her already."

"Really?! I can't believe it! Thank you!" shouted Cory.

Tara smiled. "Great. I'll grab Dr. Park, the **veterinarian**, who will examine her now. By the way, what's your dog's name?"

Cory looked puzzled. "I don't know," he said. He turned to the little pup. "Well, when I saw you, it was my lucky day," he said. "So I'll name you Clover—after a lucky, four-leaf clover!" The dog wagged her tail so fast it made a thumping sound on the floor.

Another shelter worker took Clover to the vet's office. Meanwhile, Cory asked Tara more questions about the animal shelter. He learned that most of the workers were volunteers who didn't get paid. Each day, they fed and cleaned up after the animals, walked them, and played with them.

Soon, Clover was back at the front desk. "Here's a record of Clover's health exam," said Tara. "The vet said she's about three years old, has been spayed, and is in great shape. The only thing she needs is a bath! Clover really is one lucky dog."

"We're lucky, too!" Cory said proudly.

15

# CHAPTER 3

# A Friend's Help

On their way home, the Davises stopped at The Dog House, a pet supplies store. They bought food, doggy shampoo, a brush, and some other grooming supplies.

"You should pick out some toys for Clover," Mom told Cory. He picked out a large plastic bone and a blue rubber frog. Clover jumped up and down when Cory squeezed the frog and made it squeak.

Once the family arrived home, Cory couldn't wait to spend time with his new friend. He and Clover explored the house together. It was a new home for Cory, but even newer for Clover.

"Come on, Clover!" Cory said on the stairs leading to the second floor. "I'll show you my room."

When they reached Cory's bedroom, the dog leaped on the bed. "You can't sleep here until we give you a bath!" squealed Cory.

The whole family helped bathe Clover in the backyard. Cory shampooed her fur and then gently combed out the knots. As Dad

rubbed her with a towel, Clover took off, racing around the yard like a superhero with a cape!

••• 🦴 •••

The next morning, Cory went outside to play with Clover in the backyard. He realized that he'd forgotten her favorite frog toy. As Cory turned to reenter the house, Clover raced ahead of him and ran inside. Soon, she returned with the blue squeaky frog in her mouth—as if she had read his mind!

17

Later that day, Cory decided to take Clover for a walk down the block. Her silky fur shined in the sun, and she looked like a whole new dog.

Before Clover, Cory was too shy to introduce himself to new people. But with Clover at his side, he didn't have to. People came over to him!

"What a cute dog you have!" said a neighbor wearing a big straw hat with flowers on it. She knelt down and stroked Clover's head. "Did your family just move to this street?"

"Yes. My name is Cory Davis and this is Clover. My family lives in the gray house," he said.

"It's lovely to meet you both! I'm Lydia. Welcome to Hound Town," the woman said.

"Thanks! See you later," said Cory as he continued walking. Clover happily marched down the sidewalk looking all around and occasionally sniffing the grass.

A man working in his vegetable garden stopped digging when Cory and Clover passed by. He said, "Nice dog. Can she chase away the squirrels that are eating my tomatoes?"

Cory smiled and said, "Sorry about your tomatoes. Maybe I could train her to be a garden guard dog!" The man laughed.

By the time he returned home, Cory had met five new neighbors, including a ten-year-old girl named Olivia, all thanks to Clover!

CHAPTER 4

# Into the Woods

On Saturday morning, Cory decided to take Clover on a walk to nearby Woofert's Park. "Come on, Clover," Cory said while putting on her collar and leash. "We're going to check out a new place today!"

"Mom, Dad, I'm going to the park. See you later," Cory yelled as he walked out the door.

Clover happily trotted down the sidewalk alongside Cory. When they got to the park, Cory was surprised by all the dogs he saw playing in a large grassy area.

"Wow!" Cory gasped. "No wonder this place is called Hound Town."

Cory and Clover passed a strange tan dog with very wrinkly skin. "What kind of dog is that?" Cory asked the dog's owner. "Mr. Wrinkles is a Shar-Pei." Clover and Mr. Wrinkles touched noses. "Cool," said Cory. "It's nice to meet you, Mr. Wrinkles."

Some people were tossing Frisbees to their dogs. Others were playing catch. Cory was tempted to join the crowd. But he really wanted to explore the park.

"C'mon, pal," Cory said, pointing ahead. "Let's check out the path over there."

Cory and Clover began to walk along a dirt path that cut through the entire park. Along the way, they passed a pond covered with lily pads, as well as two huge soccer fields.

The dirt path seemed to stretch on forever. Up ahead, Cory spotted a wooded area filled with tall trees and large rocks. He wondered what he might find there.

"Let's go into the woods," Cory told Clover.

They followed the path. Cory noticed some squirrels scamper up and down a tree trunk. Clover saw the squirrels, too. Suddenly, she broke away from Cory and began to chase one. "Clover, come back!" Cory called. But the dog was off and running.

As Cory raced after Clover, he tripped over a big rock in his path and fell hard on the ground. Pain shot through Cory's ankle. He tried to stand up, but it hurt too much. Cory sat on the ground, cradling his throbbing ankle.

"Clover, come back!" Cory shouted. "Please!" He didn't see the dog anywhere. In fact, Cory didn't see anyone. The woods were very quiet . . . until he heard a rattling noise.

At first, Cory wasn't sure what was making the sound. Then he saw it. A large snake with a diamond pattern along its back was coiled in the grass just a few feet away.

Cory froze. He had never seen a snake that big up close before. He remembered learning in school that rattlesnakes could be very dangerous—even deadly.

Cory wanted to run away, but with his twisted ankle, he couldn't even walk. So he sat perfectly still, and watched in fear as the snake continued to shake the tip of its tail.

Suddenly, a furry brown creature **bolted** past Cory. It was Clover! She stood directly between Cory and the snake. Then she lowered her head and began barking loudly. *Woof! Woof!* The snake rattled again.

But Clover **snarled** angrily at the creature.

Cory couldn't believe how brave his little dog was. Every time the snake moved, Clover barked and snarled.

Finally, a person jogging nearby heard Clover's barks. Cory called out, "Help, please! I hurt my ankle. And there's a rattlesnake!"

The jogger used his cell phone to call for help. He stayed near Cory but was too afraid of the snake to come closer. Now all they could do was wait . . . and hope that help would arrive in time.

# CHAPTER 5

# Stray to Star!

The next few minutes seemed liked hours. Cory sat motionless on the ground, staring at the rattlesnake. The snake coiled its long body. Clover continued to bark whenever the snake moved. At one point, the rattler struck out at the dog. Clover quickly leaped out of the way.

Finally, Cory and the jogger heard a police **siren**. "Don't worry, help is here," the jogger said with a sigh of relief.

Soon Police Officer Meg Moore and an **animal control officer** arrived. Officer Moore slowly walked toward Cory. "Are you okay?" she asked.

"Yes. I fell and hurt my ankle," Cory replied. "And my dog has been protecting me from the rattlesnake."

Officer Moore said, "Okay. Very slowly, I'm going to help you stand up. Then Officer Jake will capture the snake. That snake is **venomous** and needs to be removed from the park."

After Officer Moore got Cory back on his feet, the animal control officer took a long pole with a grasper at the end and moved it toward the rattlesnake. The snake tried to bolt. The officer quickly grabbed it with the pole, lifted it up, and dropped the rattler into a large fabric sack that he held with his other hand.

Officer Moore gently examined Cory's ankle. "I think it's just a bad **sprain**, but let's get you to a doctor to make sure. I'll have your parents meet us there."

"Okay. Can Clover ride in the police car with me?" Cory asked.

"Sure!" said Officer Moore. "Clover is the star of the day. We all have her to thank for keeping you safe from that rattler!"

Cory's parents arrived at the doctor's office just as Cory was getting out of the police car. They hugged their son tightly. The doctor examined Cory's ankle. She told Cory to rest it and not walk on it for several days.

Mom and Dad helped Cory into the backseat of their car. They said good-bye to Officer Moore and thanked her for everything.

As they rode home, Clover sat on Cory's lap in the backseat. Cory hugged the dog and kissed her head. Clover wagged her tail. Then she licked Cory's face—over and over again. The dog's wet tongue tickled and made Cory giggle.

"Clover, when school starts, I'm going to tell everyone how you saved me from a rattlesnake," said Cory. "I bet no one will believe how brave you are, girl."

Mom and Dad looked at each other and smiled. Cory's furry best friend curled up on his lap, closed her eyes, and peacefully slept the rest of the way home.

29

# Stray to Star!
## A Shelter Dog Story

1. Why was it hard for Cory to make new friends when he first moved to Hound Town? Give at least two reasons.

2. Name three ways that Clover helped Cory in the story.

3. Imagine that Cory later learns that Clover wandered away from home and really belongs to someone who wants her back. What do you think Cory should do?

4. Why do you think it's a good idea to adopt an animal from a shelter?

**adopts** (uh-DOPTS)  takes into one's family

**animal control officer** (AN-uh-muhl kuhn-TROHL AWF-uh-sur)  a person who catches stray animals

**animal shelter** (AN-uh-muhl SHEL-tur)  a place that houses homeless or lost animals

**bolted** (BOLT-uhd)  moved suddenly

**chorus** (KOHR-uhs)  a group of singers

**commanded** (kuh-MAND-id) gave an order

**commitment** (kuh-MIT-muhnt)  a promise to do something

**groomed** (GROOMD)  brushed and cleaned

**matted** (MAT-id)  covered with tangles

**meekly** (MEEK-lee)  gently

**microchip** (MYE-kroh-chip) a tiny electronic device used to store information

**pace** (PAYSS)  a certain speed

**siren** (SYE-ruhn)  a machine on a police car that makes a loud sound to warn people

**snarled** (SNARLD)  growled while showing one's teeth

**spayed** (SPAYD)  surgically altered to prevent a female dog from having puppies

**sprain** (SPRAYN)  to twist and injure a body part

**stray** (STRAY)  an animal without a home or owner

**temperament** (TEM-pur-*uh*-muhnt)  a person's or animal's nature

**venomous** (VEN-*uh*-muhs) containing venom, or poison

**veterinarian** (*vet*-ur-uh-NAIR-ee-uhn)  a doctor who takes care of animals

## About the Author

Meish Goldish is an award-winning author of more than 300 books for children. His book *City Firefighters* won a Teachers' Choice Award in 2015. He especially enjoys writing fiction, nonfiction, and poetry about animals. Growing up in Tulsa, Oklahoma, Meish liked to play with the many dogs in his neighborhood. Now a resident of Brooklyn, New York, he continues to frolic among the friendly canines there.

## About the Illustrator

Frank Scherbarth was born in Hamburg, Germany. His teachers and family noticed his artistic talent quite early and sent him to a special school to study fine arts. In the beginning of his career, Frank had to do various jobs to earn money. Eventually, he became an illustrator for magazines and newspapers. Frank has also worked as an art teacher and as a storyboard illustrator. This is his first children's book.